FAITH

HOLLYWOOD
AND VINE

JODY HOUSER | FRANCIS PORTELA | MARGUERITE SAUVAGE

CONTENTS

Collection Cover Art: Jelena Kevic-Djurdjevic
(main and BAM variant editions);
Colleen Coover (Hastings variant edition)

Editor: Tom Brennan
Editor-in-Chief: Warren Simons

VALIANT.

Peter Cuneo
Chairman

Dinesh Shamdasani
CEO & Chief Creative Officer

Gavin Cuneo
Chief Operating Officer & CFO

Fred Pierce
Publisher

Warren Simons
VP Editor-in-Chief

Walter Black
VP Operations

Hunter Gorinson
Director of Marketing,
Communications & Digital Media

Atom! Freeman
Director of Sales

Matthew Klein
Andy Liegl
John Petrie
Sales Managers

Josh Johns
Associate Director of Digital Media and Development

Travis Escarfullery
Jeff Walker
Production & Design Managers

Tom Brennan
Editor

Kyle Andrukiewicz
Editor and Creative Executive

Peter Stern
Publishing & Operations Manager

Andrew Steinbeiser
Marketing & Communications Manager

Danny Khazem
Editorial Operations Manager

Ivan Cohen
Collection Editor

Steve Blackwell
Collection Designer

Lauren Hitzhusen
Editorial Assistant

Rian Hughes/Device
Trade Dress & Book Design

Russell Brown
President, Consumer Products,
Promotions and Ad Sales

Geeta Singh
Licensing Manager

When a car accident left her orphaned, Faith Herbert was raised by her loving grandmother and found comfort in comic books, science fiction movies, and other fantastic tales of superheroes. In her teens she would discover her fantasies were reality when it was revealed she was a psiot — a human being born with incredible abilities. Imbued with a telekinetic ability to fly and a companion field that allows her to physically move objects, Faith joined a group of fellow psiots called the Renegades to stand against the forces of evil. She's since left her Renegade family behind to take on the world's challenges on her own. She may have a lot to learn about the superhero game, but if there's one thing she's always had, it's...

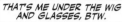
THAT'S ME UNDER THE WIG AND GLASSES, BTW.

A HERO OUT ON HER OWN FOR THE FIRST TIME NEEDS AN ALTER EGO.

AND IF THINGS REALLY WORK OUT, I'D LOVE TO INTRODUCE YOU TO MY PARENTS AND SHOW YOU WHERE I HID THE BODIES.

YOU'RE SO SWEET!

RAP
RAP
RAP
RAP

HI, I'M SUMMER SMITH, YOUR NEW NEIGHBOR OVER IN 211. JUST WANTED TO SEE IF EVERYTHING IS...OKAY HERE?

OH! SORRY!

MY IMPROV COACH SAID I NEED TO GET OUT OF MY HEAD MORE SO WE SWITCHED OUR REHEARSALS TO EARLY MORNING.

OR YOU KNOW, PRE-CAFFEINATION.

WHY WOULD YOU REHEARSE IMPROV? SHOULDN'T IT BE, YOU KNOW, IMPROVISED? COULD BE A COVER STORY.

GOTCHA. BREAK A LEG!

NOTHING LIKE A POSSIBLE MURDER TO GET YOU UP AND GOING...

...JUST ANOTHER MORNING IN SUNNY LOS ANGELES.

THE TRUTH IS, I'M STILL GETTING USED TO QUIET MORNINGS.

MY LIFE WAS PRETTY CRAZY FOR A WHILE THERE.

I ACQUIRED THESE NUCLEAR WARHEADS TO HELP US TAKE CARE OF OUR SPIDER PROBLEM.

GOOD THINKING!

RADIOACTIVE SPIDERS. HEH.

I'D ALREADY WRITTEN OFF OUR SECURITY DEPOSIT ANYWAY.

OF COURSE, THERE WERE A FEW HITCHES IN THAT PLAN...

...C'MON, LOOK ALIVE, PEOPLE.

LIKE THE FACT JOURNALISM ISN'T REALLY A THING ANYMORE. I DID LAND A JOB AT ZIPLINE, AT LEAST.

ALL MY FANDOM BLOGS OVER THE YEARS? UNDER A SCREENNAME. SO IT WAS EASY FOR SUMMER SMITH TO PUT THEM ON HER RÉSUMÉ.

10 more actors named Chris who should play superheroes on the big screen

PUBLISHED BY
TONY FEJZULA

AFTER BEING A SUPERHERO, YOU'D THINK WRITING SILLY WEBSITE POSTS WOULD BE A CAKEWALK.

SUMMER! HOW IS THE CHRIS PIECE COMING ALONG?

ALMOST DONE, BOSS.

BUT I CAN'T REALLY TELL MIMI THAT QUIZZES AND LISTICLES AREN'T AS IMPORTANT AS, SAY, SAVING THE WORLD.

YOUR RESHARE NUMBERS HAVE BEEN PRETTY LOW THIS WEEK. WE NEED TO GET THOSE UP, HMM?

SHE'S A BIT... INTENSE ABOUT THESE THINGS AS IT IS.

YOU GOT IT.

REMEMBER, THE TEAM IS COUNTING ON YOU! DON'T LET THEM DOWN!

DON'T WORRY. UNTIL SHE'S LIVESTREAMING YOUR EXECUTION, YOU'RE NOT IN *REAL* TROUBLE.

AND THE VIEWER NUMBERS WERE PRETTY LOW FOR THE LAST WRITER BEHEADING.

PAIGE IS COOL BUT A BIT HARD TO READ. SHE JOKES A LOT. (I THINK THEY'RE JOKES.)

DOES ANYONE EVEN CARE ABOUT SUPERHERO MOVIES ANYMORE? IT'S THE SAME CRAP OVER AND OVER.

WYATT IS OUR POP CULTURE INTERN. HE HATES POP CULTURE. HAD A GRADUATION REQUIREMENT TO FILL, THOUGH.

WHO LET *HIM* LOOSE?

I THINK HE JUST NEEDS A HUG OR SOMETHING.

THANK YOU FOR YOUR VALUABLE THOUGHTS ON THE MATTER, WYATT.

YOU CONTINUE TO PROVE YOU ARE INDEED THE ENEMY OF FUN.

JAY WAS THE ONE WHO TRAINED ME WHEN I FIRST STARTED HERE LAST MONTH. HE'S PRETTY CUTE.

ALL RIGHT, *HATERFACE77*, LOOKS LIKE YOU NEED TO BE TAKEN DOWN A FEW NOTCHES. *AGAIN.*

HE'S ALSO A GOOD EXAMPLE OF WHY YOU SHOULDN'T READ THE COMMENTS.

I STILL MISS MY TEAM A LOT. *THE RENEGADES!* SUPERPOWERED PSIOTS USING THE GIFTS WE HAVE TO FIGHT FOR THE LIGHT SIDE, WATCHING EACH OTHER'S BACKS!

IT WAS ALMOST LIKE HAVING A REAL FAMILY.

BUT MY COWORKERS? DEFINITELY PART OF MY PILE OF GOOD THINGS.

TONIGHT, SPARKS FLY WHEN TORQUE AND SYDNEY HIT THE TOWN ON *SOMETHING TO TORQUE ABOUT!*

REALLY?

SOMETHING WE AGREE ON.

TORQUE GOT THE REALITY SHOW GIG HE WANTED.

COME ON, BABE. YOU REALLY HAVE TO TRY IT ON A THIRD TIME?

I HEARD HE'S SEEING SOMEONE TOO. I...HAVEN'T REALLY BEEN WATCHING. FEELS TOO MUCH LIKE SPYING ON MY EX. EVEN WHEN HE *WANTS* EVERYONE TO WATCH.

YOU DON'T WANT ME TO LOOK GOOD?

UH. WHAT'S THE RIGHT ANSWER?

MAYBE SHE'S REALLY NICE. THEY ALWAYS EDIT THESE SHOWS TO MAKE PEOPLE LOOK BAD, RIGHT?

WHY HAVEN'T WE SKEWERED THIS STUPID SHOW YET?

ARE YOU WILLING TO MARATHON IT?

POINT.

BESIDES, HIS FANBASE IS WORSE THAN BIEBER'S.

WELL, IF YOU WOULD STOP BAITING THEM...

I WAS THE ONE WHO LEFT. I DON'T THINK I GET TO BE DISAPPOINTED IN HIS CHOICES.

YOU SEE THE TWEETS ABOUT FAITH BEING SPOTTED OVER THE 405 THIS MORNING?

YEAH. WONDER WHAT THAT MEATHEAD THINKS ABOUT HIS *EX* BEING BACK ON THE SCENE.

ZEPHYR'S IN L.A.? COOL.

NICELY PLAYED. VERY SUBTLE.

STANCHEK BLAH BLAH BLAH B...

ANYWAY, I COULD HAVE GONE THE REALITY SHOW ROUTE. BUT THAT WAS NEVER WHAT I WANTED.

...AH BLAH BLAH BLAH BLAH BLAH BLAH AND *UNITY*

anything cool happening??? :D :D :D

FAITH, BLAH BLAH BLAH BLAH...

I WANT TO FLY LIKE NO ONE'S WATCHING. I WANT TO HELP PEOPLE.

...BLAH BLAH BLAH BLAH *HARADA.*

all quiet.

PSIOTS. BLAH

IT SHOULD BE ABOUT SAVING THE DAY, NOT BEING THE CENTER OF ATTENTION.

...FIND OUT WHAT ZEPHYR'S UP TO, WHAT HAPPENED BETWEEN HER AND TORQUE, WHY SHE LEFT HER FELLOW HEROES BACK EAST...

I MEAN, SHE HELPED SAVE THE WORLD FROM A PSYCHOPATH, RIGHT? WHERE DO YOU GO AFTER THAT? WHO IS *FAITH HERBERT* NOW?

WE'RE THE ENTERTAINMENT DEPARTMENT, REMEMBER? NOT OUR KIND OF STORY.

SEE, THEY UNDERSTAND.

I'M TRYING TO DO MORE THAN JUST SMILE FOR THE CAMERAS AND BE SOME CELEBRITY STORY.

HAVE A GOOD WEEKEND!

IT'S NOT THAT CRIME MAKES ME HAPPY. IN A PERFECT WORLD, I WOULDN'T HAVE TO WORRY ABOUT SAVING ANYONE.

--SPOTTED A LIGHT BLUE VAN LEAVING THE RESIDENCE. SUSPECT IS--

BUT THIS ISN'T A PERFECT WORLD. FAR FROM IT.

AND AS LONG AS I CAN DO SOMETHING TO MAKE IT BETTER, I WILL.

BESIDES, BURGLARS AREN'T EXACTLY SOMETHING YOU NEED A WHOLE SUPERHERO TEAM TO DEAL WITH.

HMM. SEEMS QUIET.

puppynappers. srsly.

you have to have something for an old teammate to look into. pleeeeeaaaaaase @x? ._.

no names

may have something tho

remember the hack that exposed harada

duh, we kicked his butt and saved the world

THAT MAKES IT SOUND SO EASY. LIKE PEOPLE DIDN'T GET HURT. LIKE WE DIDN'T LOSE A FRIEND.

BUT WE HAD TO FIGHT AND WE HAD TO WIN. AND THAT'S THE THING TO REMEMBER.

tried to scrub the names of the potential psiots he'd been tracking

innocents who couldn't help what they are.

five have gone missing, no trace

whoever's behind it covered their tracks deeper than i can dig

WHOA. @X KNOWS WHAT HE'S DOING. BUILT THE WHOLE SUMMER SMITH IDENTITY FOR ME. IF HE HIT A DEAD END...

any clues??

last ping from missing kid's phone

sam bradshaw. sixteen.

worth checking but be careful

obvs!

gone two weeks with no signs anywhere

WHA--

ESCAPE WAS A FUTILE GESTURE.

WE AREN'T DONE WITH YOU TWO YET.

NO!

THERE'S STILL MUCH TO DO. CRIMES TO BE ANSWERED FOR.

THEY MAY HAVE MADE CONTACT. I'LL MAKE SURE NO TRACE WAS LEFT BEHIND.

SAM BRADSHAW SIXTEEN.

MAYBE HE WAS JUST VISITING A FRIEND AND IT'S ALL A BIG MISUNDERSTANDING.

THIS DOESN'T SEEM LIKE A PLACE WHERE MAYBE-PSIOT KIDNAPPERS WOULD HIDE.

(PRE-PSIOTS? POTENTIALS? I'LL HAVE TO WORK ON THAT.)

NO. @X ISN'T STUPID. IF HE'S ACTUALLY WORRIED, THERE'S SOMETHING BIG GOING ON.

AND I'M GOING TO FIND OUT WHAT.

DEFINITELY WEIRD. MOVING IN OR MOVING OUT?

OR NEVER HERE AT ALL?

HASN'T BEEN COLD ENOUGH TO NEED A FIRE...

GOTCHA.

I BET THIS IS THE PHONE @X TRACED. SO WHAT HAPPENED TO ITS OWNER?

WHAT ARE YOU DOING HERE?

THANK YOU. I THOUGHT SHE GOT OUT. I THOUGHT SHE...

THANK YOU.

OH, UH, NO PROBLEM.

SHE DOESN'T QUESTION WHY HER FRIENDLY NEIGHBORHOOD ZEPHYR IS EVEN HERE.

NONE OF THEM THINK TO ASK IF I HAD ANY PART IN THIS.

MISS HERBERT? WE'LL NEED A STATEMENT FROM YOU.

OF COURSE, OFFICER.

DETECTIVE.

BECAUSE THEY BELIEVE I'M A HERO.

THEY TRUST ME. THEY KNOW HOW THE STORY IS SUPPOSED TO GO.

THERE WAS THIS GUY WITH SOME SORT OF DEVICE. BEFORE THE HOUSE BLEW UP, I MEAN.

I DIDN'T GET A GOOD LOOK AT HIM, BUT THERE'S NO WAY HE SURVIVED...

ALL THESE PEOPLE OUT HERE DID, THANKS TO YOU.

AND THAT MEANS I NEED TO TRY HARDER. I HAVE TO FIND A WAY TO MAKE THIS RIGHT.

I DON'T HAVE TO FACE THIS ALONE.

COME ON, YOU TWO.

...SINCE IT'S ONLY REFLECTED SUNLIGHT, YOU DON'T HAVE TO WORRY ABOUT UV AND SKIN CANCER AND STUFF.

SO BRILL.

WELCOME HOME.

THERE YOU GO...

...JUST LIKE YOU LEFT IT.

NO, JUST HAD TROUBLE SLEEPING LAST NIGHT. I--

SINCE YOU'RE TOO SLEEPY TO CONTRIBUTE A POST IDEA, I'LL JUST HAVE TO *ASSIGN* YOU SOMETHING.

IT WAS SUGGESTED WE SHOULD DO A TAKEDOWN OF THAT SUPER KID'S REALITY SHOW. ONLY NO ONE SEEMS WILLING TO *WATCH* IT.

I'VE GOT A BAD FEELING ABOUT THIS...

...SOMETHING TO TORQUE ABOUT?

THAT'S THE ONE. I WANT TO SEE YOU *REALLY* GET YOUR CLAWS OUT.

MARATHON HOURS AND HOURS OF MY EX-BOYFRIEND'S NEW LIFE TO KEEP FROM BLOWING MY COVER?

NO. NO WAY. ABSOLUTELY NOT.

...SURE THING, BOSS.

FINE.

IT'S OKAY.

I CAN DO THIS.

I'M A FRAKKIN' SUPERHERO.

CLIK

GONNA KEEP SAYING THAT UNTIL IT'S TRUE.

AND WHO ARE YOU WEARING TONIGHT?

GIVENCHY.

CAN YOU BELIEVE I FOUND THIS AT THE MALL?!

I HAVE TO REMEMBER, THIS IS WHAT HE WANTED.

CLIK

YUR SOOOOOO PRETTY HOT, BABE. LIKE THE BEST BABE IN HERE...

OH MY GOD, WHAT'S WRONG WITH YOU? YOU'VE ONLY HAD HALF A DRINK!

EVERYTHING OUT THERE FOR THE WORLD TO SEE. THE DARK SIDE AND THE LIGHT.

CLIK

CAN YOU BELIEVE THAT POOR FROM THE BACK TRIED TO USE OUR BATHROOM?! UGH, SO GROSS.

C'MON, POOR PEOPLE HAVE TO PEE, TOO, RIGHT?

MOSTLY THE DARK.

I'M PRETTY SURE MIMI IS ACTUALLY A SUPERVILLAIN AND THIS ENTIRE JOB IS AN INTRICATE GAME OF MENTAL TORTURE.

HANGING IN THERE?

LIKE A GRAPPLING GUN.

I KNOW I'M SUPPOSED TO RIP HIM APART--BUT IT JUST MAKES ME SAD MORE THAN ANYTHING.

ALL THE POWER AND POTENTIAL AND THIS IS WHAT HE DOES? HE COULD BE SO MUCH MORE THAN THIS!

MAYBE HE JUST NEEDS THE CHANCE...

...I DON'T NEED TO END UP ON A WORST TAN LINES LIST AGAIN.

YEAH, YEAH.

NOT TOO LIKELY, AND NOT JUST BECAUSE I'VE NEVER MET CHRIS CRISWELL.

WHO THE *HELL* IS THAT?

UH OH.

UH. HI. CAN WE TALK FOR A MINUTE? ALONE?

YEAH, WHATEVER.

I GUESS SOMEONE'S NEVER HEARD OF CALLING FIRST.

SO... HOW HAVE YOU BEEN.

FAMOUS. SHOULDA STUCK AROUND, HUH?

THAT'S NOT REALLY MY THING.

LOOK, SOMEONE OUT THERE IS HUNTING DOWN POTENTIAL PSIOTS FROM HARADA'S LIST. I THOUGHT YOU MIGHT WANT TO HELP.

WHY?

WHY? BECAUSE YOU WERE A HERO, TORQUE. YOU HELPED SAVE THE WORLD.

YOU'RE REALLY GOING TO THROW ALL THAT AWAY?

SAVED THE WORLD, GOT MY REWARD. AWESOME DIGS, HOT BABE ON MY ARM, FAME AND FORTUNE...

WHY WOULD I WANT TO GIVE THAT UP?

BECAUSE I THOUGHT MAYBE YOU WERE BETTER THAN ALL OF THIS.

BECAUSE PEOPLE DIED STOPPING THE ORGANIZATIONS THAT WERE HUNTING DOWN PSIOTS.

OR HAVE YOU ALREADY FORGOTTEN CHARLENE?

I THINK ABOUT HOW FLAMINGO--CHARLENE-- SACRIFICED HERSELF TO SAVE OUR TEAM THAT DAY.

AND NO MATTER HOW MUCH HE'S CHANGED, I'M SURE HE DOES TOO.

...I THINK YOU SHOULD LEAVE.

THAT WAS A LOW BLOW, I KNOW, BUT SOMETIMES PEOPLE NEED TO HEAR IT.

YOU HAVE MY NUMBER IF YOU CHANGE YOUR MIND.

SERIOUSLY, THAT'S YOUR EX? YOU REALLY TRADED UP.

...SHUT UP, SIDNEY.

SO, THAT DIDN'T GO WELL.

I GUESS I'M ALONE IN THE FIELD FOR NOW.

@X IS GREAT, BUT HE'S MORE OF A "STAY IN THE CLOCK TOWER" GUY.

BESIDES, HE'S ALREADY DONE A BUNCH OF THE LEGWORK.

MAYBE IT'S TIME FOR ME TO PUT AWAY THE COSTUME AND PUT ON MY INVESTIGATOR HAT.

I SHOULD GET AN ACTUAL INVESTIGATOR HAT.

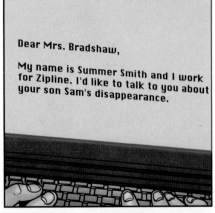

Dear Mrs. Bradshaw,

My name is Summer Smith and I work for Zipline. I'd like to talk to you about your son Sam's disappearance.

BUZZ

"THANK YOU FOR COMING, MISS SMITH."

NO ONE IN THE PRESS WAS VERY INTERESTED IN HEARING ABOUT SAM BEFORE THIS.

I'M SORRY.

I DIDN'T TELL HER I WAS A LOWLY CONTENT WRITER AND NOT A REPORTER.

I LET HER BELIEVE I WAS WRITING A STORY. IT'S FOR THE RIGHT REASONS, BUT IT'S STILL A LIE.

IF I DON'T FIND HIM AND NO ARTICLE GOES UP, IT WILL BREAK HER HEART.

OF COURSE I SPOKE TO THE POLICE. BUT THEY ACT LIKE HE RAN AWAY. GOT IN SOME KIND OF TROUBLE.

HE'S NOT THAT KIND OF BOY. YES, HE SNUCK OUT OF THE HOUSE THAT NIGHT. BUT HE'S NEVER DONE THAT BEFORE.

DO YOU KNOW WHY?

I'M NOT SURE. HE WENT OUT WITH FRIENDS OVER THE WEEKEND TO SOME SPACE T.V. SHOW THING.

BUT THE POLICE TALKED TO THEM AND THEY DIDN'T KNOW *ANYTHING*.

...WHICH TV SHOW?

SOMETHING WITH STARS. OR NIGHT MAYBE.

NIGHT SHIFTERS.

THAT'S THE ONE! ALWAYS ARGUING ON THE TWITTERS ABOUT IT...

I SHOULDN'T BE SURPRISED SAM WAS A FAN. **NIGHT SHIFTERS** IS THE HIGHEST-RATED SCI-FI COMEDY OF THE FALL.

AND THEY DO HAVE STEALTH EVENTS FOR FANS--WHICH I APPARENTLY MISSED! BECAUSE SUPERHEROING AND DAY JOB AND UGH.

BUT IT MAKES YOU WONDER. IF HE WAS ACTIVE IN THE NIGHTIE COMMUNITY, HAVE I TALKED TO HIM?

DID WHOEVER IS AFTER PSIOTS GET TO HIM THROUGH FANDOM? NOT COOL.

PEOPLE SHOULD BE ABLE TO CELEBRATE THEIR LOVE FOR SHOWS **WITHOUT** BEING ABDUCTED BY CRAZY BOMBER CREEPS.

I'LL FIND YOU, SAM. I PROMISE.

"HEY. I BROUGHT YOU SOME FOOD."

YOU HAVE TO EAT.

LEAVE ME ALONE.

ARE YOU OKAY? DID THEY--

STOP PRETENDING YOU CARE!

OF COURSE I CARE, SAM! IF I COULD DO SOMETHING, I WOULD.

BUT IF YOU GET OUT AGAIN, THEY'LL KNOW. THEY'LL EXECUTE ME.

JUST GO AWAY.

...I'M SORRY.

THE DIRECTOR IS GOING TO WANT TO SEE THIS...

SIR, THERE'S BEEN A COMPLICATION.

WE HAVE SOMEONE POKING AROUND.

AND NOT JUST ANYONE. ONE OF THE PSIOTS.

WELL, IF FAITH'S SO EAGER TO FIND US, YOU MAY AS WELL BRING HER IN.

HEY SUMMER! AMAZING TAKEDOWN OF *TORQUE*. DIDN'T KNOW YOU HAD IT IN YOU.

UM, THANKS?

AND HERE I THOUGHT I WENT A LITTLE EASY ON HIM.

WOW, I'VE NEVER HAD SO MANY SHARES ON A--

WAIT. "WATCHING TORQUE FUMBLE HIS WAY THROUGH EXISTENCE IS LIKE FINGERNAILS ON THE CHALKBOARD OF YOUR SOUL"?! I DIDN'T WRITE THAT.

(WHAT DOES "CHALKBOARD OF YOUR SOUL" EVEN MEAN?!)

SOMEONE REWROTE MY WHOLE PIECE. SOMEONE...

BLAM!

I... I...I...

UGGHH...

NEXT BULLET GOES IN ONE OF YOU. WHERE'S THE PSIOT CALLED ZEPHYR?

WYATT!

SHE'S NOT HERE! WHY WOULD SHE BE HERE?!

SO, MY FIRST SOLO ADVENTURE ISN'T GOING SO WELL.

I DON'T KNOW HOW THESE CREEPS TRACKED ME TO MY DAY JOB AT ZIPLINE.

GUESS THE BAD GUYS FIGURED OUT I'M LOOKING FOR ALL THOSE POTENTIAL PSIOTS THAT HAVE GONE MISSING.

SUMMER! GET BACK FROM THERE! THEY'LL SEE--

MY COWORKERS KNOW ME AS MILD-MANNERED SUMMER SMITH. THEY HAVE NO IDEA I'M REALLY FAITH HERBERT-SLASH-ZEPHYR.

SO HOW DO I SAVE THEM WITHOUT COMPLETELY BLOWING MY COVER?

FINE. THE HARD WAY.

PROBABLY SHOULD HAVE FIGURED OUT WHAT THE HARD WAY IS FIRST...

POK POK POK POK POK POK POK

THESE GUYS DIDN'T HESITATE. A LOT MORE PROFESSIONAL THAN THOSE PUPPY THIEVES I TOOK DOWN.

GO! HURRY!

POK POK POK

BRAKKA BRAKKA BRAKKA BRAKKA BRAKKA BRAKKA

POK POK POK POK POK POK POK POK

WHO SENT YOU?

GROZIT, WHAT WOULD A GRIMDARK, TOTALLY-INTIMIDATING HERO (WHO STILL HAS A STRONG MORAL CODE AGAINST KILLING) DO?

OH. RIGHT.

MAKE THE BAD GUYS THINK I *DON'T* HAVE A STRONG MORAL CODE AGAINST KILLING.

COME ON, BOYS. WHERE WE'RE GOING, WE DON'T *NEED* ROADS.

THEY'RE... THEY JUST...

DID MY POWERS...

NO. I COULDN'T HAVE KILLED THEM. PRETTY SURE I'D KNOW IF I WAS PHOENIXING OUT.

THEY DIDN'T SEEM TO KNOW IT WAS COMING, NOT LIKE THE ONE AT THE HOUSE.

THAT MEANS SOMEONE DID THIS TO THEM. MURDERED THEM LIKE IT WAS NOTHING.

THAT'S THREE MEN WHO DIED BEFORE THEY COULD TALK. WHAT THE FRAK IS GOING ON?

LET'S HOPE THEIR FRIEND I CLOCKED WITH THE FILE CABINET IS STILL TAKING A NAP.

FRELL.

ZEPHYR! THE MAN, HE JUST...HE JUST...

SPONTANEOUS HUMAN COMBUSTION.

DID HE SAY ANYTHING BEFORE HE BLEW UP?

HE NEVER... HE DIDN'T WAKE UP.

YOU CAME OUT OF MIMI'S OFFICE.

THE ONLY OTHER PERSON IN THERE WAS SUMMER.

WHO IS THIS "SUMMER"?

OH FEWMETS.

ZEPHYR WAS HERE FOR AN INTERVIEW! I THOUGHT YOUR IDEA WAS ACTUALLY A DECENT ONE, JAY.

NO YOU DIDN'T. WE'RE NOT IDIOTS, MIMI.

BESIDES, SUMMER'S CLOTHES WERE IN A PILE ON THE FLOOR. *JUST* A TAD SUSPICIOUS.

MAYBE SHE...BECAME ONE WITH THE FORCE?

GORRAM IT.

FINE. SUMMER SMITH IS FAITH HERBERT IS ZEPHYR. HAPPY?

I KNEW THE WHOLE TIME. OBVIOUSLY.

SO HOW ARE WE GOING TO SPIN THIS? "ALTER EGO UNMASKED"? "FROM SUPER TO SNOOPER"?

WAIT, WHAT?!

SORRY SUMM--ZEPHYR. YOU CAN'T STOP THE POWER OF THE PRESS.

EXCUSE ME. I'LL BE THE ONE WHO DECIDES--

HEY!

THAT WORKS TOO.

YOU'RE AWFULLY EAGER TO PLAY THE VILLAIN HERE.

HEY, THAT'S NOT WHAT THIS IS! WE HAVE A DUTY TO INFORM PEOPLE--

REVEALING THE HERO'S IDENTITY? RUINING THEIR LIFE? DICK SUPERVILLAIN MOVE.

ISN'T IT OUR JOB AS JOURNALISTS TO SPREAD THE TRUTH? EVEN IF IT ISN'T NICE?

THIS IS GETTING OUT OF HAND...

"JOURNALISTS," HUH?

THIS DOESN'T SAY "JOURNALIST" OR "REPORTER" OR ANY OF THE OTHER FANCY LABELS YOU--

WE STILL HAVE AN ETHICAL OBLIGATION TO--

STOP.

JAY SPENCER CONTENT WR

ALTHOUGH WE NEED TO START GETTING SOME ANSWERS. AND SOON.

WORD JUST CAME IN. THE IMPLANT DETONATION WAS SUCCESSFUL. THE THREE YOU SENT AFTER THE PSIOT WERE ERASED.

WE'RE GOING TO RUN OUT OF EXTRAS AT THIS RATE...

THAT'S THREE MORE LIVES THAT HUMANITY OWES US.

TELL THEM TO PROCEED WITH THE NEXT SUBJECT. MAYBE ONE WILL FINALLY SURVIVE THE EXPERIMENTATION.

OF COURSE, DIRECTOR.

"WE WILL MAKE THEM PAY FOR ALL THEY'VE TAKEN FROM US."

PLEASE! SOMEONE HELP ME!

NO! STOP!

@X AND I ARE TRYING TO GO ABOUT THIS MORE CAREFULLY NOW. BUT CAREFUL MEANS *SLOW.*

ALL I'VE LEARNED FROM THE PROPERTY RECORD RESEARCH IS THAT I'LL NEVER BE ABLE TO AFFORD A HOUSE IN L.A.

AND WORK HAS COMPLETELY GONE INTO BIZARRO TERRITORY. I THOUGHT THE SECRET IDENTITY WOULD LAST MORE THAN A FEW WEEKS.

"SUMMER"... THAT A NOD TO SCOTT OR BUFFY?

KIND OF BOTH, REALLY.

AND "SMITH" FOR A CERTAIN DOCTOR, I'M GUESSING?

DON'T YOU GUYS HAVE DEADLINES? BECAUSE I HAVE DEADLINES.

I CAN'T BRING MYSELF TO READ THE COMMENTS ON THE TORQUE PIECE THAT MIMI "PUNCHED UP."

EVERYTHING ELSE ASIDE, HE WAS MY FRIEND. I DON'T WANT TO SEE IF PEOPLE AGREE WITH THE AWFUL THINGS SHE SAID.

JAY SAID THE COMMENTS ON THE ZEPHYR PIECE ARE PRETTY NICE, BUT NOT READING THOSE EITHER.

FOR THE FIRST TIME THE WHOLE SECRET IDENTITY ACTUALLY FEELS LIKE A LIE.

WE STILL DON'T KNOW HOW MUCH TIME WE HAVE. IF WE'RE EVEN ASKING THE RIGHT QUESTIONS.

LOOKS ALL CLEAR HERE, @X.

OKAY. NEXT ADDRESS IS...

I THOUGHT WAITING A WEEK OR MONTH OR THREE YEARS FOR THE NEXT PIECE OF THE STORY HAD MADE ME A PATIENT PERSON.

OF COURSE, THAT WAS WHEN I ONLY HAD *FICTIONAL* PEOPLE TO WORRY ABOUT.

FAI-- SUMMER...

NEVER MIND.

WAIT, WHY IS *SHE* ALLOWED TO TAKE A NAP?!

"HAVE YOU FOUND OUT MORE ABOUT THOSE THUGS WHO SHOT UP OUR OFFICE?"

THE POLICE WERE HARDLY HELPFUL.

I'M WORKING ON IT WITH, UH, A FRIEND. THEY'RE REALLY GOOD AT COVERING THEIR TRACKS...

MMM. I GUESS JUSTICE DOESN'T HAVE A DEADLINE.

THAT'S...ACTUALLY A PRETTY GOOD LINE. I SHOULD REMEMBER THAT ONE.

ANYWAY, I GOT AN INTRIGUING INTERVIEW REQUEST TODAY. YOUR RECENT POSTS HAVE GARNERED SOME REAL ATTENTION.

I KNOW, JAY TOLD ME ABOUT THE COMMENTS HE--

HADLEY SCOTT. FROM *NIGHT SHIFTERS*. WANTS ME TO INTERVIEW HER.

I TAKE IT YOU'RE FAMILIAR WITH THE SHOW?

THE FUTURE'S A DIRTY PLACE. SOMEONE'S GOT TO KEEP IT CLEAN!

...MAYBE A LITTLE BREAK IS JUST WHAT I NEED.

IT'S SUCH AN HONOR TO MEET YOU!

ACTUALLY SUMMER, SINCE YOU'VE MET ZEPHYR, I WAS HOPING YOU COULD DO ME A FAVOR...

WOW, I HAD NO IDEA YOU GUYS HAD EVEN HEARD OF ME!

WE'RE HUGE FANS OF HOW YOU SAVE THE WORLD AND PUPPIES AND STUFF!

WE'D LOVE TO HAVE YOU GUEST-STAR ON THE SHOW!

YOU SHALL NOT PASS!

• TV •

THANK YOU, CHRIS CRISWELL.

YOU DESERVE IT, FAITH!

I'D LIKE TO THANK THE ACADEMY FOR PRESENTING ME WITH THIS FIRST-EVER AWARD FOR A TELEVISION CAMEO.

I'M JUST SO HONORED THAT--

THAT...

"HE CONVINCED EVERYONE THAT OUR PEOPLE DESERVED REVENGE. SO MANY OF OUR KIND HAVE DIED AT THE HANDS OF HUMANITY.

"WHEN THE LIST OF THE POTENTIAL PSIOTS WAS LEAKED, HE DECIDED THEY WOULD BE THE PERFECT WEAPON TO STRIKE BACK.

"HE USED ME TO LURE IN THAT BOY BECAUSE HE WAS A FAN. AND NOW THEY'RE HURTING HIM..."

I JUST DON'T KNOW WHAT TO DO ANYMORE. YOU'RE THE ONLY ONE THEY--

YOU SAID "THEY" WANT REVENGE. ON WHO?

ON EVERYBODY. ALL OF HUMANITY.

ON HUMANITY? ARE YOU SAYING YOU'RE NOT...

ARE YOU REALLY A TIME-TRAVELING CYBORG FROM THE FUTURE?

OF COURSE NOT. DON'T BE SILLY.

I'M AN ALIEN.

"THIS STUPID CRAP IS SOME REAL CRAP!"

"SO THESE ALIENS, THE VINE, CAME TO EARTH THOUSANDS OF YEARS AGO. THEY KIDNAPPED SOME PEOPLE AND LEFT THESE HUMAN-LOOKING VINE CALLED *PLANTINGS* BEHIND.

(THAT REMINDS ME, WE TOTALLY NEED TO ADD *2001* TO YOUR LIST OF THINGS TO WATCH.)

"THE PLANTINGS TOOK POSITIONS OF POWER IN POLITICS, BUSINESS, *MEDIA,* LIVING AMONG US PEACEFULLY.

"AT LEAST UNTIL ONE OF THE BIGWIG PLANTINGS IN HOLLYWOOD FORMED THIS CRAZY MURDER CULT.

"I GUESS THEY'RE MAD ABOUT THE REGULAR ALIEN VINE WHO CAME TO EARTH AND GOT THEIR BUTTS KICKED?

"ANYWAY, THEY'RE THE ONES WHO'VE BEEN KIDNAPPING POTENTIAL PSIOTS.

"DOES THAT PRETTY MUCH SUM IT UP, HADLEY?"

"IT'S ALMOST A NEW MOON, SO THE LUNAR BATHERS WON'T BOTHER SITTING OUT TONIGHT."

THIS ACCESS CARD SHOULD GET YOU INSIDE AND INTO ANY AREA YOU NEED.

WAIT... AREN'T YOU COMING WITH US?

YOU DON'T UNDERSTAND. IF THEY FIND OUT I HELPED YOU, I'D BE CUT OFF. EXCISED FROM THE HIVE-MIND.

I'D NEVER BE ABLE TO JOIN IN THE GATHERING AGAIN. I'D...BE ALONE.

SO YOU'RE ONLY WILLING TO TRY TO REDEEM YOURSELF TO A POINT--

HADLEY. REMEMBER THE MID-SEASON FINALE OF *NIGHT SHIFTERS?* THE CONCLUSION OF THE "GREAT ROBOT GENOCIDE" THREE-PARTER?

...YES. IT WAS THE FIRST TIME I DID MY OWN STUNTS.

CLICK!

COME ON. LET'S GO.

I THINK I JUST LEVELED UP IN INSPIRATIONAL SPEECHIFYING.

MOST PEOPLE WILL BE ASLEEP. EARLY CALL TIMES TOMORROW.

THERE ARE GUARDS, THOUGH...

DON'T WORRY...

I SHALL GET THIS.

CRUNCH! POW! CLANG!

GYAH!

CRASSH! SCRUNCH!

HE'S PRETTY GOOD, HUH?

YEAH.

GOTTA... SNAP OUT OF IT...

MIND CONTROL DEVICE. IF I CAN JUST...

SAW THE REAL HIM WHEN...WE WERE TOGETHER...

NOT JUST... THE SHELL... EVERYONE ELSE SEES...

...REACH INSIDE HIS PSIOT PROJECTION...

...FIND THE REAL JOHN TORKELSON... IN THE ILLUSION...

...FIND THE REAL HIM...

OLLY WO

BE... PRECISE...

YOU HAVE NO RIGHT TO ISSUE ORDERS, HUMAN. DO YOU HAVE ANY IDEA HOW MY PEOPLE HAVE SUFFERED BECAUSE OF YOURS?

THAT DOESN'T EXCUSE HURTING MY PEOPLE!

THE VINE BURNED! WE WERE SLAUGHTERED BY THE THOUSANDS! HUMANITY OWES US BLOOD!

YOU DARE TURN OUR GREATEST WEAPON AGAINST US? WE'LL DO THE VERY SAME THING TO YOUR PSIOTS.

WE WILL SEE JUSTICE!

FIRST OFF, THESE ARE PEOPLE, NOT WEAPONS.

AND SECOND, JUSTICE AND REVENGE AREN'T THE SAME THING.

SHE'S RIGHT, EVERYONE. GOING DOWN THIS ROAD WON'T HELP THE VINE.

IT WILL ONLY HURT INNOCENT PEOPLE. PEOPLE YOU'VE LIVED AMONG IN PEACE FOR--

OH SCREW HUMANITY!

THEY'VE POISONED THIS PLANET AND THEIR OWN MINDS FOR TOO LONG! DISGUSTING ANIMALS, ALL OF THEM.

WE'RE A PART OF THIS PLANET. BUT WE'RE NOT ALONE, ARE WE?

(UM, WHY IS MY REALITY STAR GIRLFRIEND IN A REALLY ANGRY CULT?)

HADLEY AGREED TO PROVIDE TESTIMONY TO G.A.T.E. I HOPE SHE'LL BE OKAY.

NIGHT SHIFTERS HAD JUST BEEN RENEWED, TOO...

TORQUE LIKED ONE OF MY FACEBOOK POSTS. I GUESS THAT'S A START.

WE NEVER FOUND SIDNEY.

I HOPE...

I HOPE HE'S OKAY.

@X IS... WELL, @X.

I KNOW HE'S ALWAYS WATCHING MY BACK, WHETHER HE'LL ADMIT IT OR NOT.

AS FOR ARCHER...

I'M QUITE GLAD I MADE THE TRIP OUT HERE. WE SHOULD DO THIS AGAIN AT SOME POINT.

STOP ALIENS WHO'VE INFILTRATED THE ENTERTAINMENT INDUSTRY FROM DESTROYING HUMANITY?

IF NEED BE.

WE COULD ALSO TRY OUT THAT DANCING SUGGESTION OF YOURS.

I'D LIKE THAT.

...ALSO A START OF SORTS.

IT TURNS OUT THAT SAVING THE WORLD ISN'T ALWAYS A LIFE-ALTERING EXPERIENCE.

(DOES THIS COUNT AS SAVING THE WORLD? AT *LEAST* L.A., RIGHT?)

NO NEW SUPERTEAM. NO FANCY MEDAL CEREMONY WHERE THEY DISS THE WOOKIEE.

JUST BACK TO THE DAY JOB I'M RELIEVED I WASN'T FIRED FROM.

BUT MAYBE THAT'S OKAY.

SORRY! HOT LIQUID!

IT'S FINE. MY BAD.

OH, FAI-- SUMMER... I WANTED TO ASK...

MY GIRLFRIEND AND I ARE PUTTING TOGETHER AN *R.P.G.* GROUP. HAVEN'T SETTLED ON A SYSTEM YET, BUT IF YOU'RE INTERESTED...

MAYBE IT'S THE LITTLE CHANGES THAT END UP BEING THE BEST ONES.

COUNT ME IN.

FAITH #1 VARIANT COVER
Art by KANO

CGC UNIVERSAL GRADE

9.8

Faith #1

Valiant, 1/16

Valiant x CGC Variant Edition

WHITE Pages

Jody Houser story
Francis Portela & Marguerite Sauvage art
Clayton Henry cover

100017239643

Faith "Zephyr" Herbert, first solo series debut

FAITH #1 VALIANT X CGC REPLICA VARIANT
Art by CLAYTON HENRY with BRIAN REBER

FAITH #1 COVER B
Art by MARGUERITE SAUVAGE

FAITH #2 VARIANT COVER
Art by COLLEEN COOVER

FAITH #3 COVER B
Art by EMANUELA LUPACCHINO
with ULISES ARREOLA

FAITH #4 COVER C
Art by CLAYTON HENRY with BRIAN REBER

FAITH #3 VARIANT COVER
Art by COLLEEN COOVER

FAITH #1, p. 12
Art by FRANCIS PORTELA

FAITH #1, p. 13
Art by FRANCIS PORTELA

FAITH #1, p. 15
Process art by FRANCIS PORTELA
and MARGUERITE SAUVAGE

FAITH #1, p. 16
Art by FRANCIS PORTELA

FAITH #2, p. 6
Art by FRANCIS PORTELA

FAITH #2, p. 10
Process and final (facing) art
by FRANCIS PORTELA

FAITH #3, p. 3
Art by FRANCIS PORTELA

FAITH #3, p. 5
Art by FRANCIS PORTELA

FAITH #3, p. 15
Art by MARGUERITE SAUVAGE

FAITH #3, p. 17
Art by MARGUERITE SAUVAGE

FAITH #3, p. 18
Art by MARGUERITE SAUVAGE

ARCHER & ARMSTRONG

Volume 1: The Michelangelo Code
ISBN: 9780979640988

Volume 2: Wrath of the Eternal Warrior
ISBN: 9781939346049

Volume 3: Far Faraway
ISBN: 9781939346148

Volume 4: Sect Civil War
ISBN: 9781939346254

Volume 5: Mission: Improbable
ISBN: 9781939346353

Volume 6: American Wasteland
ISBN: 9781939346421

Volume 7: The One Percent and Other Tales
ISBN: 9781939346537

ARMOR HUNTERS

Armor Hunters
ISBN: 9781939346452

Armor Hunters: Bloodshot
ISBN: 9781939346469

Armor Hunters: Harbinger
ISBN: 9781939346506

Unity Vol. 3: Armor Hunters
ISBN: 9781939346445

X-O Manowar Vol. 7: Armor Hunters
ISBN: 9781939346476

BLOODSHOT

Volume 1: Setting the World on Fire
ISBN: 9780979640964

Volume 2: The Rise and the Fall
ISBN: 9781939346032

Volume 3: Harbinger Wars
ISBN: 9781939346124

Volume 4: H.A.R.D. Corps
ISBN: 9781939346193

Volume 5: Get Some!
ISBN: 9781939346315

Volume 6: The Glitch and Other Tales
ISBN: 9781939346711

BLOODSHOT REBORN

Volume 1: Colorado
ISBN: 9781939346674

Volume 2: The Hunt
ISBN: 9781939346827

Volume 3: The Analog Man
ISBN: 9781682151334

BOOK OF DEATH

Book of Death
ISBN: 9781939346971

Book of Death: The Fall of the Valiant Universe
ISBN: 9781939346988

DEAD DROP

ISBN: 9781939346858

THE DEATH-DEFYING DOCTOR MIRAGE

Volume 1
ISBN: 9781939346490

Volume 2: Second Lives
ISBN: 9781682151297

THE DELINQUENTS

ISBN: 9781939346513

DIVINITY

ISBN: 9781939346766

ETERNAL WARRIOR

Volume 1: Sword of the Wild
ISBN: 9781939346209

Volume 2: Eternal Emperor
ISBN: 9781939346292

Volume 3: Days of Steel
ISBN: 9781939346742

WRATH OF THE ETERNAL WARRIOR

Volume 1: Risen
ISBN: 9781682151235

FAITH

Volume 1: Hollywood and Vine
ISBN: 9781682151211

HARBINGER

Volume 1: Omega Rising
ISBN: 9780979640957

Volume 2: Renegades
ISBN: 9781939346025

Volume 3: Harbinger Wars
ISBN: 9781939346117

Volume 4: Perfect Day
ISBN: 9781939346155

Volume 5: Death of a Renegade
ISBN: 9781939346339

Volume 6: Omegas
ISBN: 9781939346384

HARBINGER WARS

Harbinger Wars
ISBN: 9781939346094

Bloodshot Vol. 3: Harbinger Wars
ISBN: 9781939346124

Harbinger Vol. 3: Harbinger Wars
ISBN: 9781939346117

Omnibuses

Archer & Armstrong:
The Complete Classic Omnibus
ISBN: 9781939346872
Collecting ARCHER & ARMSTRONG (1992) #0-26,
ETERNAL WARRIOR (1992) #25 along with ARCHER
& ARMSTRONG: THE FORMATION OF THE SECT.

Quantum and Woody:
The Complete Classic Omnibus
ISBN: 9781939346360
Collecting QUANTUM AND WOODY (1997) #0, 1-21
and #32, THE GOAT: H.A.E.D.U.S. #1,
and X-O MANOWAR (1996) #16

X-O Manowar Classic Omnibus Vol. 1
ISBN: 9781939346308
Collecting X-O MANOWAR (1992) #0-30,
ARMORINES #0, X-O DATABASE #1, as well
as material from SECRETS OF THE
VALIANT UNIVERSE #1

Deluxe Editions

Archer & Armstrong Deluxe Edition Book 1
ISBN: 9781939346223
Collecting ARCHER & ARMSTRONG #0-13

Archer & Armstrong Deluxe Edition Book 2
ISBN: 9781939346957
Collecting ARCHER & ARMSTRONG #14-25,
ARCHER & ARMSTRONG: ARCHER #0 and BLOOD-
SHOT AND H.A.R.D. CORPS #20-21.

Armor Hunters Deluxe Edition
ISBN: 9781939346728
Collecting Armor Hunters #1-4, Armor Hunters:
Aftermath #1, Armor Hunters: Bloodshot #1-3,
Armor Hunters: Harbinger #1-3, Unity #8-11, and
X-O MANOWAR #23-29

Bloodshot Deluxe Edition Book 1
ISBN: 9781939346216
Collecting BLOODSHOT #1-13

Bloodshot Deluxe Edition Book 2
ISBN: 9781939346810
Collecting BLOODSHOT AND H.A.R.D. CORPS #14-23,
BLOODSHOT #24-25, BLOODSHOT #0, BLOOD-
SHOT AND H.A.R.D. CORPS: H.A.R.D. CORPS #0,
along with ARCHER & ARMSTRONG #18-19

Book of Death Deluxe Edition
ISBN: 9781682151150
Collecting BOOK OF DEATH #1-4, BOOK OF DEATH:
THE FALL OF BLOODSHOT #1, BOOK OF DEATH: THE
FALL OF NINJAK #1, BOOK OF DEATH: THE FALL OF
HARBINGER #1, and BOOK OF DEATH: THE FALL OF
X-O MANOWAR #1.

Divinity Deluxe Edition
ISBN: 97819393460993
Collecting DIVNITY #1-4

Harbinger Deluxe Edition Book 1
ISBN: 9781939346131
Collecting HARBINGER #0-14

Harbinger Deluxe Edition Book 2
ISBN: 9781939346773
Collecting HARBINGER #15-25, HARBINGER: OME-
GAS #1-3, and HARBINGER: BLEEDING MONK #0

Harbinger Wars Deluxe Edition
ISBN: 9781939346322
Collecting HARBINGER WARS #1-4, HARBINGER
#11-14, and BLOODSHOT #10-13

Ivar, Timewalker Deluxe Edition Book 1
ISBN: 9781682151198
Collecting IVAR, TIMEWALKER #1-12

Quantum and Woody Deluxe Edition Book 1
ISBN: 9781939346681
Collecting QUANTUM AND WOODY #1-12 and
QUANTUM AND WOODY: THE GOAT #0

Q2: The Return of Quantum and
Woody Deluxe Edition
ISBN: 9781939346568
Collecting Q2: THE RETURN OF QUANTUM
AND WOODY #1-5

Rai Deluxe Edition Book 1
ISBN: 9781682151174
Collecting RAI #1-12, along with material from RAI
#1 PLUS EDITION and RAI #5 PLUS EDITION

Shadowman Deluxe Edition Book 1
ISBN: 9781939346438
Collecting SHADOWMAN #0-10

Shadowman Deluxe Edition Book 2
ISBN: 9781682151075
Collecting SHADOWMAN #11-16, SHADOWMAN
#13X, SHADOWMAN: END TIMES #1-3 and PUNK
MAMBO #0

Unity Deluxe Edition Book 1
ISBN: 9781939346575
Collecting UNITY #0-14

The Valiant Deluxe Edition
ISBN: 9781939346986
Collecting THE VALIANT #1-4

X-O Manowar Deluxe Edition Book 1
ISBN: 9781939346100
Collecting X-O MANOWAR #1-14

X-O Manowar Deluxe Edition Book 2
ISBN: 9781939346520
Collecting X-O MANOWAR #15-22, and UNITY #1-4

X-O Manowar Deluxe Edition Book 3
ISBN: 9781682151310
Collecting X-O MANOWAR #23-29 and ARMOR
HUNTERS #1-4.

Valiant Masters

Bloodshot Vol. 1 - Blood of the Machine
ISBN: 9780979640933

H.A.R.D. Corps Vol. 1 - Search and Destroy
ISBN: 9781939346285

Harbinger Vol. 1 - Children of the Eighth Day
ISBN: 9781939346483

Ninjak Vol. 1 - Black Water
ISBN: 9780979640971

Rai Vol. 1 - From Honor to Strength
ISBN: 9781939346070

Shadowman Vol. 1 - Spirits Within
ISBN: 9781939346018

HARBINGER

Read the origin and earliest adventures
of the sky-soaring Zephyr!
From New York Times best-selling author
JOSHUA DYSART
And Harvey Award nominated artist
KHARI EVANS

"One of the most binge-worthy superhero comics
currently available..." – The A.V. Club

HARBINGER WARS

The smash-hit crossover event colliding the Harbinger Renegades
with the cutting-edged commando called Bloodshot!
From acclaimed writers
JOSHUA DYSART & DUANE SWIERCZYNSKI
And all-star artists
CLAYTON HENRY & PERE PÉREZ

"★★★★★... It's a big event done right." – Comic Vine

THE DEATH-DEFYING
DOCTOR MIRAGE

A breathtaking, heartbreaking journey
into the realms of the unknown!
From Eisner Award-nominated writer
JEN VAN METER
And visionary artist
ROBERTO DE LA TORRE

"Stunning." – io9

Faith

VALIANT

VOLUME TWO: CALIFORNIA SCHEMING

BECAUSE YOU DEMANDED IT...THE HIGH-FLYING HERO THAT CAPTURED THE IMAGINATION OF THE WORLD IS BACK WITH A COLOSSAL NEW COMICS MILESTONE!

In a city under siege by robots, aliens, monsters, and even worse... celebrities, there is only one woman the people of Los Angeles can count on: the stratospheric superhero called Faith! Aspiring reporter by day and dedicated crime-fighter by night, Faith has tackled every obstacle in her path with confidence - like those crushing deadlines at work, the long-distance boyfriend half a world away, and the missing back issues that plague her comics collection! But, unbeknownst to her, Faith is about to collide with the one force she never saw coming: an up-and-coming super-villain bent on snuffing her out once and for all! But who is lurking behind the mask of her new foe...and could they just be the one person capable of rendering Faith powerless?

Faith's headline-grabbing adventures continue here as breakout writer Jody Houser (*Orphan Black*) and sensational artists Pere Pérez (ARCHER & ARMSTRONG) and Marguerite Sauvage (*DC Comics Bombshells*) deliver the next high-flying chapter to the all-new ongoing series read 'round the world!

Collecting FAITH (ONGOING SERIES) #1-4.

TRADE PAPERBACK
ISBN: 978-1-68215-163-1

JODY HOUSER | PERE PÉREZ | MARGUERITE SAUVAGE

CALIFORNIA SCHEMING

Faith

VALIANT